TUFF,

SADIE

&

THE

WILD WEST

TUFF, SADIE

&

THE WILD WEST

Hideout Kids Book 1

by

Mike Gleason

Illustrated by Christine Harrison

FARM STREET PUBLISHING

First published 2017 by Farm Street Publishing
www.hideoutkidsbooks.com

Paperback ISBN 978-1-912207-00-8
Hardback ISBN 978-1-912207-01-5
eBook ISBN 978-1-912207-02-2

A CIP catalogue record for this book is available from
the British Library.

Design and typesetting by Head & Heart

To Michelle and Luke,
who inspired me to write these stories
of the Wild West.

TUFF

SADIE

CONTENTS

Dear Reader

Tuff, Sadie & the Wild West is the first in the series of Hideout Kids books.

In this book you meet Tuff Brunson and his best friend Sadie Marcus, two normal children from nineteenth-century New York City. They journey into the dangerous Wild West of the American Frontier on a quest to find Muleshoe, a mystical town in Texas where only children can live. Ruling over Muleshoe is the powerful enchantress Judge Junia "June" Beak.

If you want to curl up with a good story, start curling and turn the page.

Mike Gleason

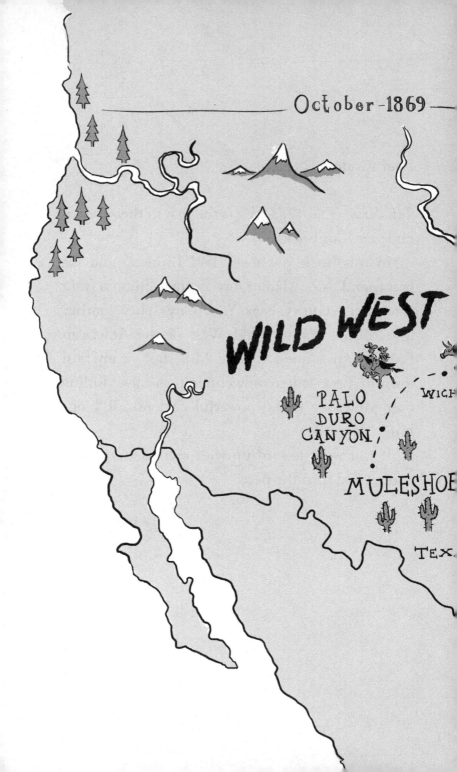

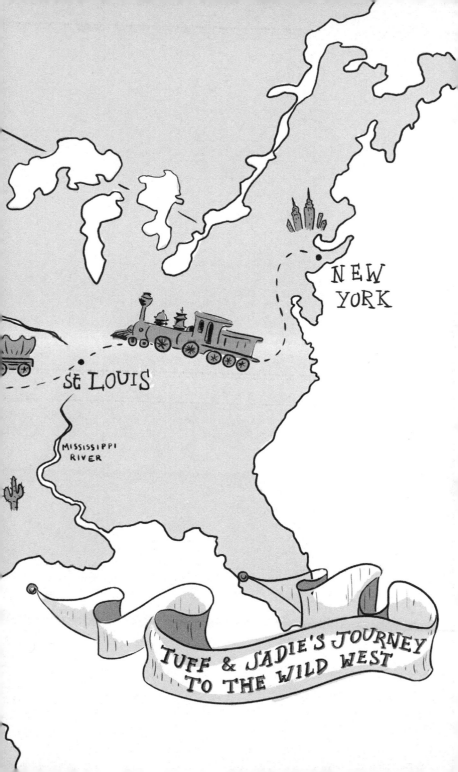

NEW YORK

S! LOUIS

MISSISSIPPI
RIVER

TUFF & SADIE'S JOURNEY
TO THE WILD WEST

CHAPTER ONE

TUFF FIGHTS HENRY

A gusty north wind whistled down Orchard Street on a rainy morning in New York City. The date was October 5th, 1869, the first cool autumn day after a long hot summer.

Ten-year-old Tuff Brunson looked out of his tiny wood and metal house. He pulled his ragged cap over his dirty brown hair, shading his freckled face.

"Tuff," his Auntie Ish said, "where are you going?"

"I have to meet somebody," Tuff said, as he stepped out of the shaky door.

He rubbed the sleep from his green eyes as red and

gold leaves and crinkled paper wrappers fluttered down the filthy street. The scent of thousands of wood fires mixed with the foul smell of horse manure that littered the road. *Phew*, he thought.

"It's about time you done showed up," a skinny blond boy said from across the street. "I was startin' ta think you were gonna chickin out. You still wantin' this waggin back?"

"Why did you steal my wagon, Henry?" Tuff said, as he edged forward. The bright red wagon Tuff used to carry Aunt Ish's groceries was parked behind the boy, whose name was Henry McCarty. "We're friends."

Not like Sadie Marcus and I are friends though, Tuff thought, wishing his best friend was with him now.

"Ain't yores," said Henry. "This waggin belongs to me. Always has."

"Not true," said Tuff. "You think it belongs to you. You think that because you saw it before I did, in the shop window. Just because you saw it first doesn't mean you own it."

"Well you ain't gonna get it back," grinned Henry, whose two front teeth stuck out like a squirrel's. "I'm keepin' it and that's that. But if you think you can take it away, well come and git it."

"My auntie worked extra hours at the factory to buy that wagon," Tuff said, drawing closer to Henry. He could smell the boy already. Henry stank. He smelled like an old rotten pumpkin.

"Then she can shore work extra hours to buy you 'nother. If you want this here waggin, yore gonna have to whup me."

"That won't be a problem. I'm happy to give you the whupping you deserve. You're nothing but a boy bandit."

Tuff stood no more than six inches from Henry's face. Henry's blue eyes had a nasty look in them.

"Go ahead and throw a punch, you robber," Tuff said, clenching his fists. "You better not miss me, 'cause it will be the last one you throw."

"You cain't whup me," Henry said. "I'm bigger than you. Yore nuthin' but a lil' varmint."

"Yes I can, wagon thief."

"No, you cain't."

"Can."

"Cain't."

"Look out you dirty outlaw. Here comes Tuff Brunson!"

Tuff jumped on Henry and they fell to the muddy road.

"Say 'give'," Tuff shouted. "Or you're getting a punch."

"I'll fight till you make me cry. That means forever," Henry said. Blood trickled from his nose.

"How's this feel you ugly thief?" Tuff said as he grabbed Henry's right arm and pulled it up behind his back. "Give up? Or should I raise this stealin' arm till it breaks?"

Tuff felt Henry's arm start to loosen. Big tears ran down his cheeks. "That's 'nuff Tuff," Henry said, whimpering. "Let me go."

"I'll let you go, for now," Tuff said as he loosened his grip. "But if you come back to this neighborhood again you'll be in for another whupping. Remember one thing your whole life: crime doesn't pay. Now get out of here."

Tuff watched Henry creeping down the road. As Henry went around the corner, he turned and hollered, "I'll remember you, Tuff Brunson. I won't forget what you did to me, for as long as I live."

"Yeah, go on Henry McCarty. I hope I've seen the last of you," Tuff yelled back.

As he turned to fetch his wagon and take it back to the shed behind his house, Tuff caught sight of Auntie Ish in the window.

Oh dear, he thought.

"Come in, Tuff," she called. "We need to talk. It's important."

CHAPTER TWO

A LETTER FROM TEXAS

Tuff pulled his red wagon into the shed. He took off his muddy boots and walked into his house.

"You know I don't approve of fighting," Auntie Ish said. "Who do you think you are, the Sheriff of New York City?"

"Henry stole my wagon," Tuff said. "I know how hard you worked to buy it for me. Should I let him take it?"

"Of course not," Tuff's auntie said. "It was wrong of Henry to take your wagon. It's also wrong to challenge him to a fight."

"OK, Auntie," Tuff said.

"Let's have a sarsaparilla," Auntie Ish said. She put her hand to her mouth as she coughed. "Please sit down."

Tuff sat on the floor next to Auntie Ish and she opened a bottle of sarsaparilla. Their one-room house was the bedroom, kitchen and living room all in one. Their only furniture was a straw bed and a rickety table. The bathroom was outside. It was called an "outhouse".

Auntie Ish doesn't look well at all, he thought.

"Tuff, I'm too sick to take care of you. You must leave New York City," his Auntie said, putting her hand on Tuff's shoulder. She coughed again. "You're going out west."

"What the –?" Tuff exclaimed. "When am I going?"

"Tomorrow," Auntie Ish said. "Please get your things packed up."

"Auntie, why do I have to leave now?" he asked. "I want to stay here; it's our home. You're sick and I have to take care of you."

Auntie Ish said, "Life should be better for children; it's why many kids are sent to the American Frontier. This is your chance."

"But who will look after you?"

"Don't worry about me. I've got a doctor coming around in a couple of days."

"Where will I go, Auntie Ish? The West is a big, mysterious place. It's wild."

"I'll tell you where," Auntie Ish said. "Do you remember my best friend, June Beak? She and I grew up together in New York City."

"I sort of remember her," Tuff answered. "She used to help you take care of Sadie and me when we were very little. Then she moved away. You told me she decided to go west, to Texas."

"That's right. I hadn't heard from her for a while but I wrote to her and told her I was sick and would like to find someone that I trust to care for you. She wrote back to me. Here's her letter," Auntie Ish said as she handed a piece of paper to Tuff. It said:

Dear Auntie Ish,

I am very sorry to hear that you are ill and can no longer care for Tuff.

Please tell him he can come and stay with me. He may bring his best friend, Sadie. I will look after them. I live in a wonderful town called Muleshoe. To find it, Tuff and Sadie must come to Texas and search for an oasis near the Palo Duro

Canyon called The Big Spring. At the oasis, they will find Muleshoe.

On the back of this letter is a map with directions on how to get from New York City to Muleshoe. They must take a steam train, covered wagons and horses.

Some people may tell Tuff and Sadie that Muleshoe doesn't exist. They shouldn't believe them.

Good luck,

Judge Junia "June" Beak,

United States District Judge of The West,

Muleshoe, Texas

"You must try to find June," said Auntie Ish. "From her letter, she's now a judge. She should be able to care for you much better than I can."

"I will, Auntie Ish," Tuff said. "I've got a map. Now I have to tell Sadie."

Tuff tore open his front door. He ran as fast as he could around the corner to Mulberry Street, where Sadie Marcus lived alone.

"Sadie, Sadie," Tuff said as he burst into her tiny shanty. "Auntie Ish is sending me away, to the West. Please come with me. I leave tomorrow."

Ten-year-old Sadie stared at Tuff with her round ebony eyes. She carefully finished brushing her straight black hair, tied it into ponytails, and smoothed her yellow dress with her strong hands.

"Where will we go?" she asked.

"We've been invited to Texas by Auntie Ish's friend June Beak," Tuff said, showing Sadie the letter.

Sadie read it carefully. "I'll come with you. I have no friends or family here but you and Auntie Ish."

"Do you have many things to bring?"

"Not much." Sadie grabbed her dice, her books and an extra dress and threw them into her rucksack.

"C'mon, let's run back to my house. I can't wait to tell Auntie Ish you're coming with me."

"Wait," Sadie said. "I have one other thing I'd like to take."

She reached under her straw bed and grabbed a beautiful golden cup. It had a silver lid which was tightly closed.

"Wow," Tuff said. "What's inside?"

"Only something I think might come in handy on the trip," Sadie replied in a soft voice.

"Where did you get it?"

"I kind of borrowed it from someone," Sadie answered. "Don't worry where I got it."

"You mean you stole it, Sadie?" Tuff said. "That's not good. I've seen you 'borrow' things before and not return them."

"Well, some things I had to sell so I could buy food. But it's not your business," Sadie said. "Let's go." They ran back to Orchard Street.

"Auntie Ish," Tuff said as they barged through his front door. "Sadie's coming with me. She's ready to go."

Auntie Ish fixed her eyes on Sadie and told her, "Are you sure, Sadie? The West is dangerous."

"What is more dangerous than a girl in New York City on her own? I can handle anything. Besides, I have Tuff. We'll protect each other."

"Auntie Ish," Tuff said as he stepped forward. "You know I always do what I'm told by you. But if Sadie doesn't come with me, I won't go. She and I will stay with you in New York City."

"OK, Tuff. June has invited you both and Sadie should go with you," Auntie Ish said. "But I don't have a lot of food to send. You'll have to share the little bit I've got."

"We will," said Tuff and Sadie.

"Also, there are rules," added Auntie Ish. "My first rule for you, Sadie, is that you need to stop

'borrowing' things from people. If something doesn't belong to you, leave it alone. Remember the bracelet you 'borrowed' from me?"

"I do," Sadie said, looking down at the floor. "I promise to get you a new one."

"Very well, then," Auntie Ish said. "I don't want you to leave each other's sides. The trip will be dangerous. My most important rule is that it's easier to *stay* out of trouble than to *get* out of trouble. Remember that."

"OK, Auntie," both children answered.

While Sadie helped Auntie Ish prepare some food, Tuff packed up his own things. He thought, *What's going to happen to us? This is scary. But we must go. Auntie Ish can't look after us anymore.*

CHAPTER THREE

THE MYSTERIOUS SINGING COWBOY

The next morning Tuff woke to the sound of the laughing seagulls. They sang "hahahahaha...ha..ha.. ha...haaaa" as they circled the nearby East River and looked for breakfast.

He woke Sadie with a little nudge to her shoulder. "Ready," she said as her eyes popped open.

Tuff jumped up from the soft spot on the floor where he slept and shook Auntie Ish, who coughed as her eyes slowly opened. "Auntie, we're ready to go west," Tuff said. "June's map shows we first take a train to St. Louis, on the Mississippi River."

"OK," said Auntie Ish. "Let's hurry to catch

your train. Here's some money for the tickets, for wagon tickets when you reach St. Louis, and for food if you run out." She handed a small purse to Tuff. "Guard it carefully."

Tuff helped her to her feet and all three headed out the rattling door.

I probably won't see this place again, thought Tuff as Auntie Ish locked it behind them.

The travelers walked along the muddy 5th Avenue toward Grand Central Station.

"I think someone's following us," Tuff said as he glanced behind.

Sadie turned around. "Maybe so," she said. "I saw somebody duck behind a wall. I hope it's not one of the teenage gang members. Let's hurry up and get to the station."

As they turned off 5th Avenue on to 44th Street, a strange sight caught Tuff's eye. A small boy sat on a tower of cartons. He looked like a cowboy. He wore a broad-brimmed gray hat, boots and chaps. Perched beside the little cowboy was a large gray owl.

As Tuff and Sadie walked in front of him, they heard the boy's soft voice sing:

> *Tuff Brunson goes west*
> *With Sadie along*
> *What happens to them?*
> *Listen to my song*
>
> *An old friend follows*
> *They might see him soon*
> *His quick hands protect them*
> *From a thieving buffoon*
>
> *Here's something strange*
> *And yucky too*
> *All their food is cooked*
> *On dried buffalo poop*

Beware The Parrot Gang,
Big Nose George and his crew
They sometimes hang out
On the road to Muleshoe

Judge June cast a spell
To make grown-ups doubt
They only see cactus
Where children hide out

"What an odd boy," Tuff whispered. "He sang a song about us. How does he know our names or what will happen to us?"

"It's a mystery. And the owl – I've never seen an owl in New York City. But I like his song," Sadie said. "Let's get going."

They kept walking and were soon at the station where they found the right platform.

"Look, it's the 'Great Western Express'. June's map says this is our train." Tuff couldn't believe it when he saw the steam engine named *The Spirit of Mississippi* chugging mightily at the front of the train. Great puffs of white steam filled the terminal.

Tuff turned to his Auntie Ish to say goodbye. "I hope you get better soon," he said.

"Yes, please get well Auntie Ish," Sadie said.

Auntie Ish cried as she hugged them both and waved them on to a carriage. "Bye Tuff. Bye Sadie. Good luck."

The crowded train was packed with young travelers. They chattered as they guarded their things. Out of the corner of his eye, Tuff thought he saw a familiar face.

"Sadie," he whispered, "do you see someone we know?"

"Don't think so," Sadie replied, looking around. "Who do you think it was?"

"Not sure," said Tuff.

They found their seats and the train surged ahead as the steam engine hissed.

"First stop, Harrisburg, Pennsylvania," announced the conductor, who wore a shiny blue hat. He marched through the train cars and called, "Tickets please."

Tuff showed him their tickets while Sadie laid out bread with a bit of strawberry jam. "Do you think Muleshoe will be hard to find?" she asked as the hungry duo gobbled down sandwiches.

Tuff unrolled June's map. "I'm not sure. June's letter mentions an oasis in the desert called The Big

Spring and that's shown on the map." Tuff pointed to the spot. "But June also said some people might tell us Muleshoe doesn't exist. It will be hard to ask directions to it then."

"Why would people say that?" Sadie asked. "Hey, wait, didn't that singing cowboy say 'Judge June cast a spell'? Can judges usually do magic?"

"Everything about that cowboy was odd," Tuff said. "I guess we'll find out when we get there."

CHAPTER FOUR

ROBBERS ON THE TRAIN

Sadie got out her dice. She and Tuff played a game called "bird cage" as *The Spirit of Mississippi* steamed through farm fields and forests, past Zanesville, Ohio, on its way west.

"Watch this, Tuff," Sadie said, as she rolled three sixes out of the hourglass-shaped box.

"Hey, those dice are loaded," Tuff said. "You're at it again, Sadie."

"Next stop, St. Louis, Missouri, on the bank of the mighty Mississippi River," said the conductor. "The river is home to catfish, dogfish, guppies, eels, walleye, large-mouth bass, small-mouth bass, no-

21

mouth bass and a few ornery water snakes."

"That conductor must own an aquarium since he knows all those water creatures," Tuff said. "I wonder how a fish with no mouth eats?"

The train brakes squealed as the train jerked to a stop and they heard shouts. "What's going on?" Sadie asked in a worried voice. "This isn't St. Louis. We're still in the middle of the countryside."

"Put yore hands up," a deep voice growled from outside their carriage. "We're comin' in."

"Robbers," another passenger whispered as she took off her beautiful pearl necklace and prepared to hand it over. "Do what they say."

"I'm not sure I want to," Tuff said. "Bandits shouldn't take our things. They're all we have."

Two outlaws burst into the carriage. One was tall and thin, dressed in old clothes with a black bandana covering his face. The other robber wore boots and a black hat with a sheriff's badge on his vest.

"Don't worry, give us all yore money and jewelry and you won't be harmed," shouted the robber with the badge.

"But you're a sheriff," Tuff said, standing up. "Why are you robbing people?"

"Listen pipsqueak," the outlaw said as he grabbed

Sadie's rucksack. "I'm no sheriff. I'm just pretendin' to be one. That's how I stopped the train. Give me yore money."

"No," Tuff said as he grabbed Sadie's rucksack back. "You can't have our money, you filthy bandit."

"Yeah," Sadie said. She punched the bandit in the stomach. "Crime doesn't pay."

"STOP RIGHT THERE.'

A blond boy had appeared at the front of their carriage. He wore a white mask over his face and pointed a slingshot loaded with a pack of marbles straight at the bandits.

"Get off this train. Now," he said in a firm voice. "Or these marbles will have your names on 'em."

"Y-Yesss, s-sirr," the robbers stammered as they shook with fear. They quickly opened the door and dove out. The boy disappeared toward the front of the train.

After a few moments the engine chugged ahead again. Everyone in the carriage cheered. "You were very brave." The lady who had taken off the pearl necklace smiled at Tuff and Sadie.

"If that boy with the slingshot hadn't appeared things might have turned out much worse," another passenger said.

"I wonder who he was?" Tuff said. "His voice sounded like someone I know."

The train soon pulled into St. Louis. Tuff and Sadie gathered their things together and stepped off the carriage. Inside the terminal it was chaos. Thousands of passengers rushed around, some with crying babies; others carried old clothes, broken furniture and whatnots.

"Well lookee here," said a familiar voice from behind Tuff. "If it ain't Tuff Brunson. And Sadie too."

CHAPTER FIVE

HENRY JOINS TUFF & SADIE

Tuff turned around and stared right into the sky-blue eyes of Henry McCarty. Now he knew he'd been right when he thought he had recognized someone on the train back in New York.

"What are you doing here?" Tuff said.

"You told me to stay out of your neighborhood so I did. I followed you from New York City. Now here I am with you in St. Louis," said Henry. "I don't mean any harm. I thought we could be friends again now that we're out west together."

"Your voice has changed," Tuff said. "You talk more like someone nice but have you really changed?

You still smell like a barrel full of bottom burps so I know you haven't had a bath."

"I have changed," said Henry. "I want a new start. Where will you settle? The West is a big place."

"Texas," Tuff said. "Let's get out of this crowded station and work out where we go next."

Tuff, Sadie and Henry left the station and found a café nearby. The café smelled of old cooked sausages and bacon. Henry got a pack of playing cards out from his rucksack and they played a game of "Go Fish".

"Do you know where you'll settle?" Tuff asked Henry.

"No," Henry said. "But I'd like to come with you and Sadie, at least for a while. Three of us together makes six eyes. All the better to spot trouble."

"I'm sure there will be plenty of trouble, Henry," Tuff said, as he stared out into the smoky red Western sky. "We'll try to stay out of it."

Sadie pulled out a beautiful pearl necklace, clipped it around her neck and said, "What's our next move, Tuff? Let's not stay in this stinky café too much longer."

Tuff looked suspicious. "Where'd you get the necklace, Sadie?"

"Oh, um, I found it on the train," Sadie said.

"I don't think you found it. The passenger on the train must have forgotten to put it back on when the robbers left," Tuff said in a quiet voice.

"That's just what you think," Sadie said.

Tuff got out the map and checked it again. "Our next move is to find the Butterfield Overland Express, a wagon train, which will take us to Wichita, Kansas."

"So what about me?" Henry asked. "Can I come with you to Wichita?"

"Are you sure you want him to come?" Sadie whispered to Tuff. "He could be nothing but trouble."

"I think he'll be alright," Tuff said.

Tuff turned to Henry and said, "You can come with us, but you have to follow our rules."

"Rules? You mean suggestions?" Henry said, with a grin. "Don't worry. Thanks for letting me come along. I think you might find I come in handy if we meet any outlaws."

"Why is that?" Tuff said.

"Because I have this," Henry said as he reached into his rucksack.

He pulled out his slingshot and pack of marbles. Sadie gasped.

"What the –?" Tuff said. "Wait. I get it. You were the boy on the train. You scared off the robbers."

"Yeah, well, it looked like my friends needed help. If you two hadn't been brave they might have got away with their crime," Henry said.

"Where did you get the slingshot?" Sadie asked.

"From under my tent near Robbers Alley in New York City," Henry answered. "A thief left it behind when he was caught by the police. I practiced by shooting tin cans off an alley wall. I became a pretty good shot."

Henry twirled his slingshot and put it and the marbles back into his rucksack. He smiled at Tuff.

"Shall we go?" he said.

"Yep," Tuff said. "On toward Texas."

CHAPTER SIX

COVERED WAGONS TO RIDE

Sadie was the first to see the sign. "Butterfield Overland Express, Straight Ahead One Mile, Over the Eads Bridge," she called out.

They stood on the sandy bank of the mighty Mississippi River. Its fast-moving muddy water stood between them and the Stagecoach Station.

Straight ahead was the entrance to a bridge, the biggest they had ever seen. The thick wooden trestles and giant arches soared over the swift river. The bridge looked like a giant brown grasshopper stuck above the murky water.

"Look," Tuff said. "There's an elephant walking

across the bridge. Let's catch up with him. I've never seen one."

The three friends dashed for the bridge entrance past thousands of people trying to get a look at the bridge and the elephant.

"What's going on?" Sadie asked an official in a blue uniform.

"You don't know?" the official said. "Well, that is a 'test elephant'. This bridge was finished yesterday, after seven years of building. We send an elephant across first because they won't set foot on an unsafe structure. If he stops the bridge isn't safe."

"Look at his trunk," Sadie said. "It's amazing."

"An elephant's trunk comes in handy for almost everything," the official said. "He uses it for drinking, eating, smelling, lifting, breathing, and for protection."

"Let's follow the elephant," Tuff said. "I've never seen an animal that big."

"Yeah, if he slows down, let's find some peanuts to feed him," Henry joined in. "That will keep him moving."

Tuff, Sadie and Henry followed the elephant as he stepped across the new Eads Bridge over the mighty Mississippi River. He dropped massive piles of gooey poop every few steps. "Phew, does that stink," Sadie said as she pinched her nose. "I can't even smell you anymore, Henry."

The elephant tiptoed daintily all the way across.

"It's safe. The Eads Bridge is open," the official

pronounced. "Come one, come all."

"We were the first to cross," Sadie said.

"There's the Butterfield Overland Express," Tuff said.

Their mouths dropped open as they saw the "prairie schooners" for the first time. In front of them stood three bright-red covered wagons, with "Concord Coaches" painted in white on the side. The spokes of the wooden wheels were as tall as they were.

Teams of enormous oxen and mules grunted and lowed as they munched on bales of hay.

"Let's ride those wagons," Tuff said.

CHAPTER SEVEN

BULLWHIPS AND A SLINGSHOT

"Excuse me, sir," said Tuff as he approached the scruffy driver of the lead wagon. "The three of us are Tuff, Sadie and Henry. We're from New York City. We're on our way to the town of Muleshoe, in Texas. Can we ride with you?"

"Muleshoe? There isn't a town called Muleshoe," the Driver said. "People talk about it, but no grown-up has ever seen it. Hey Shorty, we got three city kids who want to go to Muleshoe. What do ya think? Should we give them a ride?"

From behind the wagons walked "Shorty". He was massive, as big as a giant. He had filthy tanned skin that was covered in dust and mud. "He looks like an ox," Tuff mumbled to Sadie.

"Smells like one, too," Sadie said.

"Whoa," said Henry to Shorty. "You're not short at all. You're huge."

"I guess, by the same reasoning, your name must be 'Handsome'. 'Cause you're not handsome at all, you're ugly," said Shorty to Henry.

The Driver laughed. Then the oxen laughed at Shorty's joke. Even the mules laughed at the joke.

Tuff looked over at Henry. He didn't laugh. He had a nasty look in his blue eyes. His hands reached into his rucksack.

"No, Henry," Tuff said in a low voice.

"Look," Shorty said, when the laughing had stopped. "This wagon train can take you to Wichita. Then you can get horses to take you to Texas. Good luck finding Muleshoe. People say it's near an oasis in the desert, but everybody I know who's been to that oasis says they only see a forest of giant prickly pear cactus around it."

"Legend says a powerful witch put a curse on the oasis. The cacti are supposed to be poisonous," the Driver said. "There ain't a town around there."

"We're not worried about curses. We'll take our chances," Tuff said as he looked at Sadie.

"Then let me show you tenderfoots how everything works," Shorty said. "I'm the lead bull-whacker, and my job is to keep the oxen or mules, whichever we have pullin' the train, movin'. This here's my whip."

Shorty unrolled the biggest whip Tuff had ever seen. The solid wood handle was three feet long and the braided rawhide lash was twenty feet long, tipped with nine smaller lashes. They were called tails and the whip was a cat-o'-nine-tails.

"I call this 'The Persuader'." Shorty laughed as he cracked his whip.

"I'd love to learn to use one of those," Tuff said. "But I think it might be too hard for me."

"Not for me," Sadie said.

"Good," said Shorty. "Because you get to try. My other bullwhackers didn't show up this morning. You can take their places, as long as you show me you can use these whips. If you can, I'll give you free tickets for the trip."

"Let's give them a try," Tuff said.

"Here you go," Shorty said as he handed two

bullwhips over to Tuff and Sadie. The Driver watched from his wagon. "You want one too, Handsome?" Shorty winked at Henry.

"Stop calling me 'Handsome'," Henry said. "Now."

"What's your name again?" asked Shorty.

"It's Henry."

"Henry," said Shorty. "That's a chicken name. You're no hen. With those two front teeth stickin' out, you look more like a billy goat. How about from now on, we call you Billy."

"I like that name," Sadie said.

"Me, too," said Tuff. "What do you think Henry?"

"Alright," Henry said, "Billy will do. I never much liked Henry."

"Watch this, New York City kids. I'll show you how to use the bullwhip," said Shorty. "I've put a silver dollar coin on that stake over there. Now I'll remove it."

"CRACK!" went Shorty's whip. The coin fell to the ground.

"Now you try," he said to Tuff as he put the coin back on the stake. "Don't be nervous."

"Here goes," Tuff said. "But I'll close my eyes. This whip is scary."

Tuff closed his eyes, whirled the whip above his head, turned around in a circle then "CRACK!" sounded his whip.

"Here you go, Shorty." Tuff handed him the silver dollar. "I guess I was lucky on my first try."

"What the –?" Shorty said. "Never seen anybody do that."

"What about you, ponytails?" Shorty said to Sadie. "Bet you can't even lift the whip. You're just a girl."

Sadie grabbed the whip and glared at Shorty as he walked over and bent down to replace the coin. "CRACK!" sang Sadie's whip.

"Oww," hollered Shorty.

"You've got a hole in the back of your trousers," Sadie said. "Here's the piece of cloth. Maybe you can ask one of your 'girls' to sew it back on for you."

"Well I'll be a frog's dinner," Shorty said. "She snapped a hole right out of my breeches. Never seen such whip work in all my days. What about you, Billy? Got any magic up your sleeve?"

"Toss that silver dollar in the air and I'll show you," Henry, who was now known as Billy, said as he lifted his slingshot out of his rucksack. Shorty

tossed the coin high above them.

"THWACK!" went Billy's slingshot and the coin fell to the ground.

"Is there a marble hole in that piece of silver?" Billy said.

Shorty looked at the hole in the coin, then at Billy's slingshot.

"I didn't even see you lift that slingshot," Shorty said. "You're the fastest I've ever seen."

The Driver hollered and laughed. "Hey, Shorty," he said. "You're the slowest on the draw I've ever seen and now I've seen the fastest."

"What have they been eatin' up there in New York City?" Shorty said to the Driver.

"Looks like all of us have 'Persuaders'," Tuff said with a smile.

"Now look here," Shorty said as he pointed at three teenage boys sitting on top of the second wagon. The boys held long Winchester rifles. "These three are scouts, looking out for danger. They shoot deer, antelope and buffalo. Outlaws too, in case we should come across any."

"Along this trail is a band of dangerous outlaws," the Driver explained. "Their leader's name is Frank Smith but he calls himself 'Fast Bull'. His father was a Mountain Man. His mother was a Cherokee Tribe Indian. He's a bad egg."

Tuff, Sadie and Henry climbed into the first wagon.

"Let's get going," the Driver said as he yelled at the oxen. "Yip, yip."

CHAPTER EIGHT

BUFFALO STAMPEDE

The Concord Coaches rolled down the trail.

"I'm hungry," Sadie said. "Think they have anything to eat on this wagon?"

A scout soon poked his head through the window. "Anybody for some antelope jerky and a drink of sarsaparilla?" he asked.

"You bet," said Tuff. "Where are we?"

"We're on the Smoky Hill Trail," said the scout. "You might want to crawl up on top of the wagon and get some sleep. It's more comfy up there. The Driver says we'll stop at Fort Fletcher. It's a US Army fort."

Tuff, Sadie and Billy grabbed blankets from the

coach storage box and went up on top of the wagon. The sun was going down in the west and the sky was filled with gold, red and purple clouds.

"The sunset is so beautiful," Sadie said. "We never saw anything like that in New York."

As the sun went down the full moon rose behind them, lighting the plains almost as brightly as the sun. A couple of tall elm trees along the trail cast long dark shadows. Huge brown clouds were moving across the light green pastures.

Except they weren't clouds.

"Buffalo," the Driver said. "Millions of them. Antelope and deer, too." His voice took on an alarmed tone. "Hey Shorty. Come up here." The Driver looked around for his lead bullwhacker. "Look over there."

Shorty quit tending to the oxen and hurried up next to the Driver. A massive herd of buffalo had broken away and were running straight toward them.

"STAMPEDE!" Shorty yelled.

"Quick," the Driver said. "Put the wagons behind me in a straight line. We'll head for that tree. It's the only way to escape a stampede."

"WHACK!" Shorty cracked his whip as he yelled at the slow-moving oxen. "C'mon you slow-footed

beasts. Help me, bullwhackers."

Tuff and Sadie grabbed their bullwhips. They lashed and snapped them as they helped drive the terrified oxen into line. "I hope I can keep this up," Tuff yelled. "This whip is so hard to control."

Billy hopped down off the wagon and helped straighten the line of trailing mules by firing his slingshot into the air then jumped back up again.

Just in time the prairie schooners managed to line up behind a huge elm tree. The thundering herds of buffalo roared past them.

"It's like being surrounded by a black cloud," Sadie shouted as she bounced on top of the wagon. "The stampeding hooves are shaking the ground."

It was over almost as soon as it had begun. Shorty tried to settle the frightened beasts.

"Whew," Tuff called up to the Driver. "That was close. They were right next to us."

"Thanks kids," the Driver said. "You were all a big help. Everybody has to pitch in when you travel across the frontier. There's always some trouble or the other."

"Phew, what stinks?" Sadie said.

Tuff crinkled his nose. "It smells like rotten eggs."

"Never smelt a skunk before?" Shorty said as he continued to calm the oxen. "He sprays that smell out of his tail when he gets scared. It makes people and animals run away. Maybe he helped chase off those buffalo."

"Are we ready to move on to Fort Fletcher?" the Driver said.

Shorty checked all the oxen were properly yoked and nodded.

"Let's move. Yip. Yip."

"Let's get some sleep," Tuff said, feeling tired now the excitement of the stampede was over. He, Sadie and Billy lay down under their blankets, listening to a few loud "hoot hoot" calls from prairie owls. They were soon fast asleep.

CHAPTER NINE

OUTLAWS ATTACK THE WAGONS

They woke as the sun peeked above the horizon. The wagon wheels groaned as the Driver brought the wagons to a halt.

"You kids must have been mighty tired," the Driver said. "You slept right through our stop at Fort Fletcher. Now we're on a short break to cook some breakfast."

The sun slowly rose as the chatty black crows sang their "caw caw caw" songs. Dark green hay fields stretched out for miles around them but close to the trail were strange holes in the ground.

"What are those holes all around us?" Tuff asked

as he and Sadie climbed down from the top of the wagon. Billy was still dozing.

"Those are wallows," the Driver answered. "When the buffalo get thirsty or hot, they burrow down in the ground, to find water. They make a shallow hole about twelve feet across. Wallows make good hiding places."

"Let's have a bit of breakfast and a sarsaparilla," Sadie said as she and Tuff joined the Driver, Shorty and the scouts around the fire where they were cooking. "What do you have, Driver?"

"I've got venison sausages and pheasant eggs, all cooked over a hot fire of buffalo chips."

"Buffalo chips?"

"Yeah, dried buffalo poop. The plains are full of it. We burn it and throw the meat right on top. Dee-lish."

"You mean the sausages sit right on top of the burnt poop?" Sadie said, looking at the fire to check it was true. "I don't think I'm that hungry any more."

"I am," Tuff said. "What about you, Billy?"

Billy was still on top of the wagon, looking out over the plains. "Hey Shorty," he said. "What does a war party of outlaws look like?"

Shorty dropped his plate and ran up to the roof.

"Turn out," he shouted. "Get ready all. Here they come! Outlaws!"

Tuff and Sadie leapt up to join him on the roof. "Oh, dear," Tuff said. "This looks bad."

In the distance they could see a long black line. It slid like a snake through the prairie hills, headed straight for them. They could already hear the outlaws' battle cries.

The Driver called out, "Let's get these wagons in a circle."

Tuff and Sadie lashed their whips above the oxen and the scouts joined Shorty as he moved the wagons into a tight circle.

By the time they had managed it the rumble of the charging horses' hooves shook the ground, like thunder after a lightning strike. The outlaws' whoops grew louder. Arrows began thumping around them.

Tuff fell backward, horrified, as their wagon jolted forward.

"My oxen," the Driver said. "They're taking off. Help, Shorty."

"CRACK!" sounded Shorty's whip as he tried to control the beasts but they continued to pull the wagon out of the circle. "They're scared. They won't be stopped."

Tuff scrambled back to his feet and he and Sadie helped Shorty get the oxen under control. By now they were fifty yards away from the other two wagons. The scouts had their rifles out. Billy already had his slingshot primed and within moments the raiders were upon them. They rode right up to the wagon, chopping at it with their knives and tomahawks.

"Quick," shouted the Driver. "Our only chance is to get out of this wagon. Let's get into that buffalo wallow."

Tuff grabbed his rucksack. He and Sadie lashed out with their whips, while Billy fired his shooter. Outlaws dropped as the brave New Yorkers fought their way to the wallow.

"Wait, my rucksack," Sadie cried. "I forgot to grab it."

"Here you go, Sadie." A large gray owl swooped down and dropped her rucksack into the wallow.

"Tuff, did you see that owl?" Sadie asked.

"I did, but we've got to hurry. C'mon," Tuff said to the Driver and Shorty. "We'll cover you."

The Driver grabbed something from the wagon and he and Shorty followed Tuff, Sadie and Billy into the wallow. "I've brought our bullwhips. Don't be afraid to use 'em," the Driver said.

"Watch out," Sadie cried. "Right above you, Tuff."

Tuff looked up to see an outlaw on the edge of the wallow, tomahawk already raised to attack him.

"CRACK!" Before Tuff could lift his own, Sadie's whip caught the tomahawk and twisted it out of the invader's grasp. As he tried to run away Tuff grabbed him, "Not so fast, bad guy." Tuff said. "POW!" He dropped the outlaw with one punch to the jaw.

"Ouch," Billy laughed. "I know how that feels."

Tuff peered out over the edge of the wallow. The remaining outlaws had circled their horses around the wallow and also formed a circle around the other wagons. The circles were growing tighter.

"They've taken over our wagon," Sadie said, joining Tuff. The outlaws were crawling all over it, like bumblebees over a hive. One of them set the canvas on fire.

Tuff said, "I'm going out. I've had enough of these bandits."

"Don't," Sadie cried, but Tuff had already dived for the Driver's box.

"Look out, you dirty outlaws. Here comes Tuff Brunson!" He gritted his teeth and grabbed his bullwhip. Circling it tightly over his head, he jumped out of the wallow. "SNAP!" "SNAP!" "POP!" "POP" the whip sang out.

"Go, Tuff," the Driver said. "The circles are breaking up."

"I snapped over their heads," Tuff said, "enough for them to think they were under a lightning cloud."

"Wait," Sadie said. "What's that noise? It sounds like music."

Over the thunder of battle, whooping, shouting, and the whoosh of arrows came the bright note of a trumpet sounding a "CHARGE"!

Shorty lifted his head out of the wallow. "It's the United States Army."

CHAPTER TEN

RESCUED BY THE US ARMY

A huge army of soldiers on dark brown horses galloped toward the outlaw war party. The crackle of rifle shots rang through the air. At the front of the charge brightly dressed Crow Tribe Indian scouts rained arrows down on the raiders.

"The Crow scouts must have heard about the attack," the Driver said. "They brought in the Army from Fort Fletcher."

The outlaws scattered and vanished over the horizon.

Sadie, Billy, the Driver and Shorty climbed out of the wallow to join Tuff.

Tomahawks and arrows littered the ground around the circled wagons. Riderless ponies wandered about. A cloud of smoke floated above the prairie.

"Howdy, folks," said a friendly soldier in a broad gray hat and blue uniform. "I'm Colonel Tumblin from the US Army, Fort Fletcher. Looks like you've had a little trouble."

"Yeah, a little," Shorty said as he grinned at the Colonel.

"We should have sent you out with an escort when you left Fort Fletcher. When our Crow Tribe scouts told us about the plans for the outlaw attack we came out right away," the Colonel continued.

"Who were those raiders, Colonel?" the Driver asked. "Was that Fast Bull?"

"Yep," said Colonel Tumblin. "Your fight was with a gang of renegade outlaws led by Frank Smith, who calls himself Fast Bull. He's a bad egg."

"Thanks, Colonel. Let's move 'em out, bull-whackers," the Driver shouted. "Tuff, Sadie and Billy ride in the second wagon. I'll be driving it since they burned ours."

"Luckily I still have this," Sadie said. She held the golden cup she had taken from under her bed in

New York City. "The owl saved my rucksack."

In her other hand Sadie held up a razor-sharp stone tomahawk. It had a blood-red painted handle. "I have war bounty as well."

"Let's go up top and enjoy the countryside," Tuff said as he, Sadie and Billy climbed aboard the second wagon. They waved goodbye to their rescuers from Fort Fletcher and the Butterfield Overland Express got underway across the frontier plains once more.

Along the trail hundreds of little prairie dogs stopped digging and watched from their mounds of rich brown dirt as the wagons wheeled past.

The autumn sun bathed the bright-red wagons in yellow light, which gave them a golden glow. Smoke from buffalo-chip fires hung in the air.

"I guess we'll get used to that smell," Tuff said.

"I won't," said Sadie. "Look, it's Wichita."

The wagons stopped for a moment at the edge of the bustling town. Thousands of

longhorn cattle walked about in pens. "MOO," they bellowed.

"Those longhorns have come up the Chisholm Trail from Texas," Shorty said as they started up again. "You're almost there."

CHAPTER ELEVEN

HORSES AND HOODOOS

When they reached the center of Wichita, Tuff and Sadie hopped down off the wagon to say goodbye to Shorty and the Driver.

"Thanks for getting us here safely," Tuff said.

"We're the ones who should thank you," the Driver said. "Now, you'll need horses to get down to Texas, won't you? Three of them? I'll go get 'em."

"Wait," Billy said as he jumped down off the wagon. "I won't need a horse. I think I'll stay in Wichita for a while."

"You want to stay here?" Sadie said. "You don't want to come with us?"

"I don't. After a few days in Wichita, I'll maybe go on to the territory of New Mexico. There might be some good chances out there, for a guy like me. I'm sure you'll hear of me again. Bye Shorty, and thanks for my new name," Billy said with a laugh. "See ya, Sadie. Bye, Tuff."

"Bye Billy," said Tuff and Sadie.

Billy walked off down the rowdy main street. His relaxed hands gently swung next to his ebony-handled slingshot.

"You know," said Shorty. "Your friend Billy, with those two squirrely buck teeth, and that blond hair, and those blue eyes, he looks like no more than a little kid."

"Yeah," said Tuff in a quiet voice. "But those blue eyes can get a real nasty look. He's got shoot in his eyes."

"Here we go," the Driver said as he walked up. "Two fine horses, saddles and saddlebags included. My present to you, for your bravery."

"Thanks," Tuff said as he and Sadie hopped up on the horses. "Hang on, these horses are backing up. They're supposed to ride straight ahead."

"Those horses are ornery but they'll move with a bit of 'persuasion'. If you find Muleshoe, let me know," Shorty laughed. "Good luck."

Both horses laughed. "We're not going all the way to Texas," they neighed.

"Oh yes you are," Sadie ordered as she and Tuff spurred them hard in their sides and galloped out of Wichita.

"It looks like we ride straight south to Palo Duro Canyon. Not far to Texas," Tuff said as he grabbed the map from his saddlebags. "Guess what? The Driver's put s'mores inside. Yum."

Sadie reached into her saddlebags. "I feel bottles of sarsaparilla," she said with a happy smile. "Yippee. Oh, and I happened to find these as well."

She pulled out two bullwhips.

"Sadie," Tuff said. "You stole those from Shorty."

"I didn't steal them, Tuff," Sadie said. "I borrowed them till we see Shorty again sometime. We might need them, for protection."

"Alright, Sadie, but please tell me next time you decide to 'borrow' something that doesn't belong to you," Tuff scolded. "We can make the Palo Duro Canyon by nightfall. Some of the hoodoos there might have caves carved under them. We can sleep in one of those caves if we find one."

Tuff and Sadie rode the trail hard all afternoon. As the sun started to set, they approached a large canyon surrounded by cliffs of yellow and brown rock. Their horses slowed and waded through a shallow copper-colored river.

"We must be in Texas now," Tuff said. "The map shows the boundary as the Red River."

The full moon rose above the cliffs.

"This is so beautiful," Sadie said. "Look, there's a cave. Let's go in."

"There's been a campfire here," Tuff said as he

climbed off his horse and touched the warm burnt logs on the ground, near the opening to the cave. "Let's get a fire going."

"This is not your cave," growled a voice from inside.

CHAPTER TWELVE

A STOP IN A COMANCHE TRIBE CAVE

Tuff and Sadie almost jumped out of their boots.

Indians, with tomahawks drawn, surrounded them.

"My name is Chief Ten Bears of the Comanche Tribe Indians. Hand me the reins of your horses," said the owner of the gruff voice as he stepped through the circle of Indians. "These are my tribal members. We will not harm you. Who are you? Where do you come from?"

"My name is Tuff Brunson and this is my friend Sadie Marcus. We come from New York City," Tuff said, handing over the reins of his horse. Sadie did the same and the surrounding Indians lowered their tomahawks.

"Where are you going?" Chief Ten Bears asked.

"We're on our way to Muleshoe, Texas, where we hope to settle," said Tuff.

"Who do you know in Muleshoe?" said Chief Ten Bears.

"We don't know anyone," said Tuff, "but we were invited there by Judge Junia –"

"June Beak," Chief Ten Bears interrupted, with a wide smile. "She is my friend, but I haven't seen her for a long time. She is very powerful. She practices magic."

"Do you know how to get to Muleshoe from here?" Tuff asked.

"No. None of our tribe has seen Muleshoe. All we know is that Judge June is supposed to live there. Legend has it that it's near an oasis called The Big Spring," Chief Ten Bears answered. "The Big Spring is surrounded by a forest of poisonous giant prickly pear cactus. We won't go near it."

Chief Ten Bears signaled to one of his Comanche. He took a headdress from him and handed it to Sadie.

"If you find Judge June, please give her this, as a token of friendship from the Comanche Tribe," said Chief Ten Bears.

"I will," said Sadie.

The Comanche stared at Sadie.

Sadie stared back at the Comanche.

"If you have come all the way from New York City, you must be hungry," Chief Ten Bears said. "Let's give you something to eat."

The tribe busily set about making food. "It's amazing how quickly they work," Tuff whispered to Sadie. "It's a good thing, too. I'm starving."

Sadie looked up at the Comanche then glanced at Tuff. The Comanche would not stop staring at her.

"Come, we will eat," said Chief Ten Bears. He took a piece of the cooked meat and held it up to the sky. Then he chanted a few words and buried it in front of him.

"To please the Great Spirit," he said. "How do you like the food? It's antelope steaks and mulberries."

"It's good," Tuff answered.

Sadie said nothing. The Comanche who kept staring at her walked over to Chief Ten Bears, bent down and whispered in his ear.

Chief Ten Bears nodded.

"The horses you have are old and no good," Chief Ten Bears said. "Our tribe would like to give you two of our horses. They're young animals, children, like you. We trained them – they were mustangs, wild horses."

The Comanche still stared at Sadie.

"I want to leave, Tuff," she whispered. "I don't like the way he is looking at me."

"OK, Chief," Tuff said, standing up. Sadie jumped up beside him. "Thank you for the meal.

Can you show us the new horses? We'd like to be on our way."

"You don't understand, Tuff," said Chief Ten Bears. "This is a trade with you. You get the horses –".

"What do you get?" Tuff asked.

"Sadie," Chief Ten Bears said. "She can have the horse but she stays here, with us."

He signaled with his hand.

The tribe formed a circle around Sadie.

CHAPTER THIRTEEN

SADIE & CHIEF TEN BEARS EXCHANGE GIFTS

Oh, dear, thought Tuff, *what can I do to get us out of here?*

"Why do you want me?" Sadie asked. "I have something much better. Something that will please you."

"What do you have, Sadie?" said Chief Ten Bears as he raised an eyebrow.

Sadie pushed through the surrounding Indians, walked over to her saddlebags and pulled out the golden cup she had brought with her from New

York City. She unwrapped the cup. A wonderful smell, like freshly baked chocolate-chip cookies, filled the air.

"This is a special potion," Sadie said. "It comes from the East. It has magical powers, to cure sickness."

"Ohhh," said Chief Ten Bears. "May I see it?"

Sadie handed him the golden cup. Chief Ten Bears opened it and tasted the potion.

Chief Ten Bears and his tribe bowed toward Sadie.

"I know this potion," he said with a deep breath. "It is wonderful. Now I understand why Judge June has invited you to come to her. You may go with Tuff. Please sleep in the cave, as our guests. Tomorrow morning you will have the horses."

The Comanche Indians led Tuff and Sadie into the cave where they lay down in a pile of leaves and quickly fell asleep.

Tuff woke at dawn to the songs of bobwhite quail outside the cave. "Bob...white," "Bob...white," they trilled.

"Sadie," he whispered as he shook her arm. "Wake up."

Sadie sat up and rubbed her eyes.

"I'm glad you brought that golden cup, even though I don't like how you got it," Tuff said as he bounded to the front of the cave. "The Comanche are gone. So are the horses we rode from Wichita. And, Sadie, come here right away. You won't believe your eyes."

Sadie rushed over to his side. Standing outside in the bright morning sunlight were two of the most glorious horses they could ever imagine.

"Tuff," Sadie said in a voice barely above a whisper. "They're looking at us."

Tuff stared at the rugged and muscled chestnut colt. He looked like he would beg Tuff to ride him. He stood tall, like a knight waiting for his squire to don his coat of armour.

"His hooves are shiny, like silver. I'm going to name him Silver Heels," Tuff said.

At the sound of his name, Silver Heels whinnied and bared his white teeth.

"He smiled at you, Tuff," Sadie said.

Next to the colt was a beautiful black mare. She stood without effort, as if she floated above the ground. She was a smooth, sparkling horse with a broad chest. She looked bored, as if she would laugh

at other horses that tried to catch her.

"She's mine," Sadie said. "I'll call her Jenny."

Jenny pawed the ground and threw her head back with a "Neigh".

Gray, polished saddles had replaced their old ones. Brand new snakeskin saddlebags lay across the horses' backs. On the saddle horns hung two wide-brimmed white felt hats.

"Look, new boots," Sadie said.

On the ground were two pairs of knee-high, brown boots, made of tough buffalo skin on the soles and soft deerskin above. The boots were decorated with red, blue and yellow streamers.

"And new chaps," Tuff said. "They're buckskin."

"You can smell the fresh leather," Sadie said as she and Tuff put on the boots, chaps and hats. "They must have been made overnight. There's a note attached to the colt."

Tuff reached up and took a piece of dirty white parchment off the big colt. He read out loud:

Dear Tuff & Sadie

Thank you for the gift of the potion.

These two horses and outfits are presents to you from Chief Ten Bears and our tribe. The horses are Comanche-trained mustangs, from our ancestral lands on the Great Plains.

When you speak to them, they listen, and do exactly what you say. They will also speak to you. These horses are children, as fast as the tornado winds. We hope you will always be friends of the Comanche Tribe Indians.

X Ten Bears

"Wow," Sadie said. "They speak to us. Should we have a s'more and a drink of sarsaparilla for breakfast, then take these ponies for a run?"

"Are you kidding?" Silver Heels snorted as he stomped his hooves. "Let's leave right now."

"We don't like hanging around," Jenny whinnied as she pawed the ground.

"Wow," said Tuff. "Looks like we hop on or they'll leave us behind."

"Here you go," Sadie said as she handed a bullwhip to Tuff. "Better keep that handy." She looped her own bullwhip around her saddle horn. "Race you down the canyon."

CHAPTER FOURTEEN

WARNING FROM THE PARROT GANG

Their horses fairly flew through the wide canyon, lined with steeple-like hoodoos, as they followed the Red River Trail south.

Tuff noticed Silver Heels' ears prick up. Jenny's ears did the same. The two horses looked at each other and whinnied.

Sadie said, "We've got company ahead. Looks like bad guys. Outlaws."

Fifty yards in front of them, in the shade of a juniper-tree grove, were three filthy horse riders. They wore black hats and outfits, with red bandanas wrapped around their necks.

"They look like some of those terrible teenage gangs back in New York City," Sadie said.

"They've each got a pair of six-shooters," Tuff said, as he reached down and fingered his bullwhip. "Let's be alert."

"I'll be ready," Sadie said. She opened her saddlebag and squeezed her fingers around the tomahawk she had taken from the battle in Kansas.

The gang had strung a thick rope across the narrow path. Tuff and Sadie reined in Jenny and Silver Heels and slowed them to a walk before stopping.

"Where are you two goin'?" sneered the biggest of the three outlaws. "Who are you, with your pretty white hats and sleek horses?"

"My name's Tuff Brunson and this is Sadie Marcus. We're on our way to Muleshoe, sir," said Tuff in a polite voice. "Now if you would please move your horses and remove this rope from across the trail, we'll be on our way."

"On your way to Muleshoe," roared the medium-sized rider. "'Sir' and 'please' he says, like a city slicker. Ha, ha, ha."

"Yeah, don't they look all prim and proper," squealed the smallest rider, a girl. "Real good boy and girl. Yuk."

"Who are you, pimple face?" Sadie said to the girl, in her strongest voice. "Not that I care. You smell like something that dropped out of your horse's bottom." Sadie stared at the filthy outlaw with her fierce black eyes.

"Grrr," snarled the grimy girl as she pulled a club out of her saddlebags. "I'm gonna pop this snotty proper girl on the head right now."

"Wait, Peggy. Put that club away," said the biggest outlaw in a voice that growled like a bear's. "Now, hi there, sugar. My name is George Parrot. This here is my brother, George, and my sister,

Peggy. Folks around here call us Big Nose George, Little Nose George and Tiny Nose Peggy. We don't know why. Ha Ha Ha. We're The Parrot Gang, meanest outlaws in the Wild West. From now on, stay out of our way. We control this whole territory, includin' Muleshoe. I used to live in Muleshoe. That town belongs to me."

"I figured out why you're called Big Nose," Tuff said with a cool voice. "You've got the biggest snout I've ever seen on an ugly teenager."

Sadie lifted the tomahawk out of her saddlebag and chopped the thick rope stretched across the trail in two.

"Catch you later, Parrot Gang," Tuff shouted as he and Sadie showed their horses the whip. They galloped out of the grove leaving The Parrot Gang covered in their dust.

"Never call me sugar again, you grisly outlaw," Sadie yelled, over her shoulder. "Or you'll regret it."

"We'll get you," coughed Big Nose George.

CHAPTER FIFTEEN

WELCOME TO MULESHOE

"That tomahawk came in handy, Sadie," Tuff said. "Good going. Did you hear Big Nose George say he used to live in Muleshoe? At least we've met someone who has been there."

"We must be getting close," Sadie agreed as they followed the trail through the brown dusty plains.

"Texas is like a desert," Tuff said. "Dry and flat with few trees or plants at all. You can see for miles all around."

"Look, there's a sign," Sadie said.

Silver Heels began to slow and Jenny followed. "I'm not reining him in," Tuff said. "He slowed on his own."

Tuff looked up. A short distance ahead of them beautiful bright green trees surrounded a small blue lake, which sparkled in the sunlight. "That must be the oasis of The Big Spring," Tuff said.

Sadie said, "Where are the giant prickly pear cacti? I only see leafy green trees."

"Me, too. Look, there's an opening in the trees.

Let's ride through. Aren't those yellow flowers on the branches beautiful?"

Tuff and Sadie rode through a shadowy archway of flowered trees. The smell of the flowers reminded Tuff of peanut-butter cupcakes, his favorite.

The shadows gave way to bright sunshine as they entered a pretty valley, which lay below gleaming round hills. A small stream of clear water trickled over moss-covered stones. A little group of old wooden buildings seemed to rise up out of nowhere.

"Look, there's a sign ahead," Tuff said. "We made it."

"At last. Let's tie the horses up here," said Sadie, pointing to a hitching post outside a bright blue painted building. "HAPPY DAYS SALOON" said the gold-lettered sign above the batwing doors. They tied Silver Heels and Jenny to the hitching post and near to a trough of water.

"Sadie, look," said Tuff, as he caught his breath in surprise. "There – on the veranda of the saloon. It's the same tiny cowboy singer we saw in New York City. And the gray owl again."

"Oh," Sadie whispered. "So it is."

The small boy sat on a rocking chair with the gray owl perched on its arm. He slowly rocked back and forth: his tiny legs stretched out with his boots propped up on the rail, his hat sat back on his head. Tuff and Sadie listened as he quietly sang:

A big warm welcome
Tuff and Sadie are here
They made it all the way
Let's give them a cheer

Muleshoe is a special place
Take a look about

It's a children-only town
All others must keep out

"Hey," Tuff said, trying to catch the boy's attention, but before Tuff had said the last syllable the boy had disappeared. "He's gone."

"I think we'll see him again," Sadie said with a smile.

"Yes, you will," said the gray owl as he slowly blinked.

The two weary travelers pushed open the batwing doors and strolled into the busy saloon. A cry rose up: "Welcome to Muleshoe Tuff and Sadie."

A beautiful girl approached them. She had long black hair, which was pulled back from her enchanting blue-gray eyes. She moved so quietly she seemed to glide across the saloon.

"That's Auntie Ish's friend June. I remember her," Tuff whispered to Sadie. "But she looks different now."

"I don't remember her at all," Sadie said.

"Hello, Tuff. Hello, Sadie," the girl said in a soft voice. "I'm Judge Junia Beak. Nice to see you again. Here everybody calls me Judge June. Welcome to

Muleshoe. We're so pleased you've arrived."

"We're pleased too," said Tuff. "It feels like a long time since we left New York."

"I hope your Auntie gets better soon. I think she will," Judge June said. "Would you care for an ice-cold sarsaparilla?"

"Yes, please," Tuff and Sadie said as Judge June glided over to the bar. Tuff and Sadie followed her.

"Look at the way she moves," Tuff whispered to Sadie. "She doesn't look like us. She doesn't walk – she kind of floats. I think she's a witch."

"Don't witches have a familiar?" Sadie whispered back. "It's usually a black cat."

They joined her at the crowded bar. "Say hello to Toothless Tom, our bartender," Judge June said as Tom put their drinks down in front of them.

As they sipped their sarsaparillas, Tuff said, "On our way here, almost everyone we met told us we wouldn't find Muleshoe. But we weren't worried. As you wrote in your letter, we didn't believe them."

Judge June smiled and said, "Since only children are allowed to live here, I made sure only children can find it. It's a place for children who don't have a home in the West. I protect them."

Tuff looked around at the ragtag group of kids,

who smiled and chatted as they sipped chocolate milk and cold sarsaparilla.

"Deputy Dan Pigeon, Toothless Tom and Jelly Roll Jim help out around town," Judge June said. "They were children here. Now they're teenagers."

"What about food and water?" Sadie said. "Who cooks for all the kids?"

"Muleshoe is a lucky town," Judge June said. "Our water comes from The Big Spring, an underground lake. It provides water for goats and buffalo, which give us our milk. We grow our own fruit and vegetables. All the kids help with the cooking. Oh, and we don't use buffalo poop to cook. You'll be happy to hear that, Sadie. Would you like to come up to my hut?"

"Sure," said Sadie.

"Let's go," said Tuff.

Judge June led them across the dusty road and pushed open a bright-yellow door into an old, wooden two-story building.

I remember. Only witches have huts, Tuff thought, with a shiver. *She's definitely a witch.*

CHAPTER SIXTEEN

JUDGE JUNE BEAK, THE GOOD WITCH

Tuff felt cool, soothing air on his face as Judge June closed the door behind them.

He glanced around the room. It was filled with piles of old books and faded maps. In a corner stood a massive stuffed black bear, with sharp claws and gleaming white teeth.

"I'm glad he's stuffed," Tuff whispered to Sadie.

Wait, did that bear wink at me? he thought.

"I understand you met my friend the Comanche Chief Ten Bears," Judge June said. "He provided you with two fast horses and new outfits."

"Yes, he gave us this headdress to give you. But

how did you know we saw him?" Sadie asked as she handed over the headdress.

Judge June smiled. Her eyes sparkled. "I have many friends in the West," she said. "They tell me things."

"Chief Ten Bears said he hadn't seen you for a long time," Tuff said. "He said you are very powerful, and practice magic."

"It's true Chief Ten Bears and I haven't seen each other for a while. I like to stay in Muleshoe," Judge June said. "I must protect the children. As for the magic, I do practice a bit from time to time. I am a witch, after all."

I KNEW IT, Tuff thought.

"So that's why grown-ups can't find Muleshoe and only see a cactus forest?" Sadie asked.

"Yes," said Judge June. "I suppose that's why. You have to believe it to see it. Muleshoe is a hideout for kids."

"If you're a witch, where's your black cat?" Sadie asked.

"Oh dear, Sadie," said Judge June as she smiled. "Not all witches have black cats. My familiar is a gray owl. I think you might have seen him a couple of times on your trip. I also

97

have a pet. Her name is Wild Thing."

"Grr," came a growl from under the table and a pink fairy armadillo crawled out.

"Oh, here she is now. Try to be polite, Wild Thing."

"I'm the boss of this town. Bring me some mash."

"Here you go, sweetheart," Judge June said, putting a bowl of smushed-up grub worms and maggots in front of Wild Thing.

"CHOMP!" went Wild Thing.

"Nice to meet you Wild Thing," said Tuff and Sadie.

"BURP!" said Wild Thing.

"Are you really a Judge?" Tuff said.

"Yes. President Ulysses Grant appointed me as a United States District Judge of the West. My job is to make sure people obey the law," said Judge June.

Why would the president appoint a witch as a judge? Tuff wondered. *She MUST be a good witch. I hope so.*

"That must be kind of hard," Sadie said.

"You're right," Judge June said. "Many people who come to the West don't behave very well. That's why it's called the Wild West. Now, Tuff and Sadie, I'm told that you care a great deal about law and order. You are both brave and honest."

"Wow," Tuff said. "You heard about our fight with Fast Bull."

"Yes," said Judge June with a scowl. "He's a bad egg."

"A rotten egg," Sadie said.

"I have jobs for you both," Judge June said. "More and more honest people are coming out west to make a new start. Since I have been appointed a judge, I need a strong sheriff to fight crime across the Wild West. Tuff, I'd like you to take the job. Will you do it?"

"Will I do it?" Tuff said as he smiled. "Yes."

"Sadie," Judge June said. "Are you willing to work alongside Tuff, as his deputy?"

"Yes," Sadie said, as a big grin spread across her face.

"Good," said Judge June. "Tuff, I will have a special belt made for you. Every time you arrest an outlaw, you'll get a golden star. When the belt is full of stars, you'll become a United States Marshal, top lawman in the West."

"I accept. I love golden stars. I don't like outlaws," Tuff said.

"Sadie," Judge June said, "I have special plans for you. A day will come when I no longer wish to carry out my duties as a judge. I heard you gave Chief Ten Bears a special potion. I know this potion, just as he does. Where did you get the golden cup that contained the potion?"

Sadie tried to answer. "I, um, uh – I borrowed it."

"I know what happened," Judge June said. "You also 'borrowed' a beautiful pearl necklace and a couple of bullwhips, didn't you?"

"Yes," Sadie said.

"I would like to teach you my customs and duties so one day you may become a District Judge of the West. For me to do that, you need to try to stop 'borrowing'. Do you understand?" Judge June said.

"I understand," said Sadie.

"Good. Congratulations Sheriff Tuff Brunson and Deputy Sadie Marcus. Let's grab lunch at the Happy Days Saloon. I'm sure you're starving."

"Yay," said Tuff and Sadie. "Here we go!"

THE END

AUTHOR'S NOTE

In this series of adventures about the Wild West, I introduce many words, things and events that my readers might not have heard before. Here are some simple explanations and definitions to help you discover and understand facts about the Wild West:

Sarsaparilla: The most popular soft drink of the Wild West. It's thought to have healing powers and is made from the root of the sarsaparilla vine. Yummy!

Elephant Bridge Test: Elephants were often used to test a new bridge when it first opened. They would not walk across unless they thought the bridge was safe. The elephant and The Eads River Bridge is a true story.

Prairie Dogs: They are not dogs at all; they are rodents, like rats. In the days of the Wild West they were the most common mammals to be found in America.

S'mores: Chocolate covered marshmallows, served

on sugar crackers. Dee-lish! "S'more" is short for "some more". They're so good you always want more.

Hoodoos: Tall, thin spires of rock found mostly in the desert. They often have caves near the ground.

Oasis: A place in a desert where water can be found.

Witch's Familiar: An animal-shaped spirit who helps a witch perform her magic.

Pink Fairy Armadillo: The smallest and hungriest of all armadillos.

GENERAL MUSTER
& NO-TREES TOWN

Chapter One
DRAW, SHERIFF

It was high noon on a boiling hot summer day in Muleshoe.

On the dusty main road, Sheriff Tuff Brunson squared his shoulders. He stood ramrod straight as he faced "Big Nose" George Parrot, the meanest outlaw in the Wild West.

Tuff stared straight into the vicious outlaw's bloodshot eyes. "I won't tolerate teenage gang members in this town," Tuff said, in a voice barely above a whisper. "Drop your water blaster and walk away. Now."

Big Nose George wiped the sweat from his brow. "Draw," he growled through his black-stained yellow teeth. "Muleshoe don't have room for the both of us."

Tuff curled his fingers around his bullwhip, hoping he would be lucky with it again this time.

"Look out, you dirty outlaw, here comes Sheriff Tuff Brunson!" he cried as he whirled the bullwhip out.

"CRACK!" He whipped Big Nose George's super soaker from its holster.

"Don't mess with the fastest whip in the West," Tuff said, hiding his relief.

Deputy Dan Pigeon pounced on Big Nose George and pulled his arms up tight behind his back.

"Put handcuffs on that ugly bandit then throw him in jail," Tuff said as he waved his bullwhip in the air. "Be careful he doesn't try anything sneaky."

"Nice one," said Tuff's deputy Sadie Marcus, as she smiled at him from beneath her wide-brimmed hat. She watched from the veranda of the Happy Days Saloon. "He didn't even get close to his squirter. Hey, look out, Tuff."

Tuff heard the scrape of boots on dust behind him. He whirled around. Big Nose George had tried to wrestle the handcuffs away from Deputy Dan.

"CRACK!" Tuff's whip leapt out. The whip curled and snapped as it wrapped in a knot around Big Nose George and pinned his arms to his side.

"Now that rascal is roped good and tight, cuff him up," Tuff said.

Deputy Dan yanked Big Nose George's wrists together, shoved them into the handcuffs and clicked them shut.

"Look at this," laughed Deputy Dan as he took Big Nose George's water gun away. "This wasn't loaded with water. He had bubble-gum instead. Watch." Deputy Dan pulled the trigger and a big pink bubble popped out of the barrel.

"I'm not surprised," said Sadie. "The Parrots are dumb."

"You might have got me now, Sheriff Brunson, but you won't keep me long in that chicken-pen jail of yours," hollered Big Nose George. "My sister 'Tiny Nose' Peggy has got a big surprise for you. You and your snotty-nosed dep-u-ty are gonna get what you deserve."

"It's not a chicken pen, it's a parrot pen. See ya later, Big Mouth Parrot," Tuff laughed, as he rolled up his whip and hung it on his belt.

"Crime doesn't pay, does it?" said Sadie with a grin. "Poor Big Nose George. He's not as scary as he thinks. Let's go get a sarsaparilla. Judge June will be in the saloon. She might have a job for us."

As Tuff and Sadie walked toward the saloon doors, the tiny cowboy poet appeared at the end of the veranda. "Look, Tuff, there's our little singing friend," Sadie whispered. The little cowboy sat in his old rocking chair, his boots propped up on the rail, as he sang,

> *Big Nose George will cry*
> *Since he's back in jail*
> *But the Parrots know*
> *It's not the end of the tale*

> *An army of outlaws*
> *Threatens Muleshoe*
> *Unless help arrives*
> *What will the kids do?*

"Hey, cowboy –" Tuff started to say, but the tiny cowboy had disappeared.

Tuff and Sadie pushed open the batwing doors and walked into the noisy Happy Days Saloon.

The saloon was crowded with Muleshoe children eating lunch. The air smelt of *cabrito* – barbequed goat. Judge Junia "June" Beak had one arm propped on the wooden bar as she talked with Toothless Tom, the bartender.

Tuff and Sadie weaved their way through the tables to Judge June, who raised her hand to stop them. "There's not time for a sarsaparilla," she said. "I have a job for you. Someone very important is coming to Muleshoe and I need to make sure he gets here safely. Let's go over to the hut and talk. There are way too many ears listening around here."

Tuff saw "Little Nose" George Parrot at a nearby table.

"What are you doing here, birdbrain?" Tuff said to him. "Would you like to join your big brother in the bird cage?"

Little Nose George took off his filthy black hat as he glared at Tuff. "You're no worry to The Parrot Gang," he snarled. "My brother will be out of jail before you can say 'boo'. Me and my sister Tiny Nose Peggy are about to take over this town. We've got an outlaw army."

"Oh, go jump in a lake, 'Little Brain' George," said Judge June. "C'mon kids, let's get over to the hut."

So far in the
HIDEOUT KIDS series...

MIKE GLEASON

HIDEOUT KIDS

TUFF, SADIE
& THE WILD WEST

MIKE GLEASON

HIDEOUT KIDS

GENERAL MUSTER
& NO-TREES TOWN

MIKE GLEASON
HIDEOUT KIDS
HONEY
HONEY
HONEY
GRIZZLY BEARS
& BEAVER PELTS

MIKE GLEASON

HIDEOUT KIDS

MACHO NACHO
& THE COWBOY BATTLE

ABOUT THE AUTHOR

Hideout Kids author Mike Gleason comes from a small town in Texas. He grew up with cowboys, cowgirls and exciting stories of Wild West adventures. He was a wildcatter in the Texas oil fields and a board director at MGM in Hollywood. He created and produced an award-winning music television series at Abbey Road Studios. He lives and writes in London.

Made in the USA
Las Vegas, NV
21 December 2020